eclares the LORD, "plans to prosper you ive you hope and a future." JEREMIAH 29:11 NIV

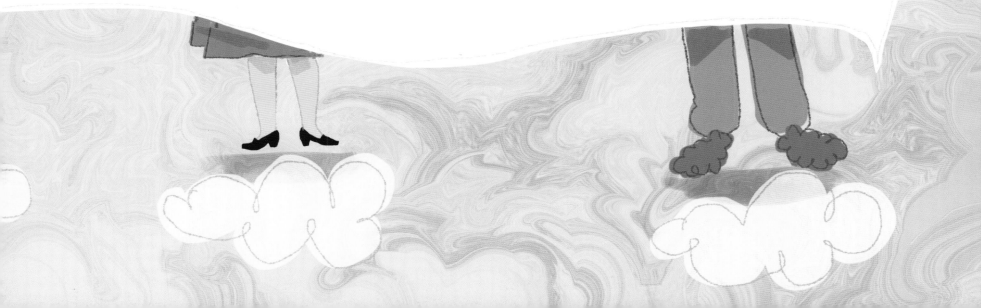

To Michael & Ethan.
May you always pursue the plans He has for YOU!
—AP

To the little church girls in my sister and me, and to children everywhere:
know that God has a plan just for YOU.
Run to your destiny and become who you already are in Him.
—VBN

ZONDERKIDZ

The Plans I Have for You

Copyright © 2015 by Amy Parker
Illustrations © 2015 by Vanessa Brantley-Newton

This book is also available as a Zondervan ebook.
Visit www.zondervan/ebooks.

Requests for information should be addressed to:

Zonderkidz, 3900 Sparks Drive SE, Grand Rapids, Michigan 49546

Library of Congress Cataloging-in-Publication Data

Parker, Amy, 1976–
      The plans I have for you / written by Amy Parker ; illustrated by Vanessa Brantley-Newton.
            pages   cm
      Summary: Illustrations and rhyming text reveal the YOU Factory, where God arms each new person
with tools to do the work that he or she was created to do, to fulfill a special purpose and make the world a
better place.
      ISBN 978-0-310-72410-0 (hardcover) – ISBN 978-0-310-73619-6 (epub)
      ISBN 978-0-310-73620-2 (epub) – ISBN 978-0-310-73621-9 (epub)
      [1. Stories in rhyme. 2. Creation—Fiction. 3. God—Love—Fiction.
4. Individuality—Fiction.] I. Newton, Vanessa, illustrator. II. Title.
PZ8.3P1645Pl 2015
[E]—dc23   2014027702

Editor: Barbara Herndon
Art direction and design: Kris Nelson

Printed in China

15 16 17 18 19 /DHC/ 12 11 10 9 8 7 6 5 4 3 2 1

The Plans I Have For You

WRITTEN BY
AMY PARKER

ILLUSTRATED BY
VANESSA BRANTLEY-NEWTON

ZONDER**kidz**

Hey, YOU!

I've got big plans
for you!

Yes, **YOU,** and you,

and **YOU** over there too!

I need **YOU** in a hospital

and **YOU** at the zoo.

YOU'll be an entomologist
in a forest in Peru.

I've given you a purpose—
it's been there *since birth!*

OHH, it's no little purpose!
(I don't do things small.)
Yours is the most

Yes, this job is for **YOU**,
   and ONLY YOU can do it!
I'm counting on YOU...

so, c'mon, get to it

YOU'll find what you need RIGHT THERE in your skin! (I thought it all through when I put that stuff in.)

Patience

Love

Helpful

Kindness

To **YOU**

I gave BIG hands,
to YOU, two BIG feet,
YOU'll be my BIG helper,
YOU'll walk down BIG streets.

I've left you instructions—
right here in my book!

So open it often—
and take a good look!

Remember that I, who made
the whole world, made YOU.
And there's nothing that,
with my help, YOU can't do!

So open your heart
and listen real close.
You'll find that one thing
that you love the most.

HELLO
YO

HOSPITAL

OCTOPUS

Then, when you do,
you'd just better watch out!
'Cause I'll send you BIG jobs
to be inspired about!

The whole world will be better,
thanks to little ol' you …
all because you did
what I CREATED **YOU** to do.

WHAT?!
You're still reading?!
There's so much to do!
Now, go out and find
my big plans for

YOU.